In memory of my mother
and her loving babysitting skills.
–H.E.B.

In memory of my dear cousin Alex.
–G.D.

KOKILA
An imprint of Penguin Random House LLC, New York

First published in the United States of America by Kokila, an imprint of Penguin Random House LLC, 2021

Text copyright © 2021 by Hilda Eunice Burgos
Illustrations copyright © 2021 by Gaby D'Alessandro

Kokila & colophon are registered trademarks of Penguin Random House LLC.
Visit us online at penguinrandomhouse.com.
Library of Congress Cataloging-in-Publication Data is available.

Manufactured in China
ISBN 9780593110478

1 3 5 7 9 10 8 6 4 2

Design by Jasmin Rubero
Text set in LTC Goudy Oldstyle Pro

The art for this book was created digitally.

The Cot in the Living Room

HILDA EUNICE BURGOS ✦ illustrated by GABY D'ALESSANDRO

Kokila

I wish I could sleep on the cot in the living room.
But Mami says it's for guests.

"What's so great about that cot?" my sister asks.

I lower my voice to a whisper. "It would be so much fun to have the whole living room to myself! I'd stay up late and play, look at the tiny cars outside, maybe watch TV and sneak into the kitchen for an extra cookie or a little dulce de leche."

My sister shakes her head.
"I just like to sleep at night."

On Friday, I help Mami snap the sheets onto the cot's comfy mattress. They're still warm from the dryer, and they smell like my bubble bath. Mami smooths over the top sheet until there isn't a single wrinkle left. She finishes everything off with one of her handmade quilts and our fluffiest pillow.

"Who's coming tonight?" I ask.

"Raquel."

Boring. She never plays with me.

Raquel's dad is working the night shift at the hospital.
So she gets to sleep on the cot in the living room.

"Do you like dominoes?" Papi asks.

"We can make a maze."

Papi never lets me build with the good dominoes.

"No, thank you,"
Raquel says in a whisper.

"Will you keep the lamp on?" Raquel asks.

"Don't worry, mi amor," Mami says.

"It doesn't get very dark in here."

I wish my room had a big window to let in the lights from the George Washington Bridge.

It's not fair.

We change the sheets again the next day. Edgardo's
mom is singing tonight. She won't finish until three a.m.
So he gets to sleep on the cot in the living room.

He'll probably get crumbs all over it again.

"Are you hungry?" Papi asks. "I can make you a snack."

I'm not allowed to bring food into my room.

Edgardo shrugs.

"Mami packed this for me."

"Do you know my mom's good-night song?"

"I don't, papito," Mami says. "But you can sing it to this little guy."

He gets a snack and my toy?!

It's not fair.

Little Lisa's grandmother drops her off on Monday after dinner.
She's cleaning offices all evening, until way past bedtime.

So Lisa gets to sleep on the cot in the living room. I hope she
doesn't wake us up in the middle of the night again.

"Do you like cartoons?" Papi asks. "I can change the channel."

But I'm watching that!

Lisa shakes her head.

When her grandmother peels her away, she sticks to Mami like cotton candy.

"I don't fit in this little bed, preciosa," Mami says. "But I'll rub your back until you fall asleep, okay?"

Mami turns off the TV and I go to my room, where there is nothing to watch.

It's not fair.

No one comes over on Tuesday.

"Can I sleep here tonight?"
I ask Mami.

"But you have your own bed."

I tell her that my sister snores. Which is true.

Mami shrugs. "Okay," she
says.

We put warm sheets on
the cot, and I smooth them
over until there isn't a single
wrinkle left.

My parents kiss me good night, then turn out the lights. I hear their bedroom door close. There's nothing good on TV now, but that's okay. This night is going to be perfect because I'm finally sleeping on the cot in the living room.

But this mushy pillow
isn't mine.

GROWL

And there are monsters in here.
Something is growling in the kitchen.

"Mamita, what's the matter?" Thank goodness Mami is back! She holds my hand and walks down the hall with me. We slip into my room and I fall asleep to the music of my sister's snoring.

It's Wednesday and Raquel's dad is working the night shift again, so she has to sleep on the cot in the living room. All by herself. She must really miss him.

It's not fair.

"There isn't much extra space in our room," my sister says.

"But there's just enough," I tell her.

She agrees.

The cot fits perfectly.
And so does Raquel.